A MESSAGE TO PARENTS

Reading good books to young children is a crucial factor in a child's psychological and intellectual development. It promotes a mutually warm and satisfying relationship between parent and child and enhances the child's awareness of the world around him. It stimulates the child's imagination and lays a foundation for the development of the skills necessary to support the critical thinking process. In addition, the parent who reads to his child helps him to build vocabulary and other prerequisite skills for the child's own successful reading.

In order to provide parents and children with books which will do these things, Brown Watson has published this series of small books specially designed for young children. These books are factual, fanciful, humorous, questioning and adventurous. A library acquired in this inexpensive way will provide many hours of pleasurable and profitable reading for parents and children.

Published by Brown Watson (Leicester) Ltd.
ENGLAND
© 1980 Rand McNally & Company
Printed and bound in the German Democratic Republic.

NUBBINS *and the* TRACTOR

The story of a farm horse

By FREDA SINNICKSON

Illustrated by CLARE McKINLEY

Cover illustration by BARBARA CLYNE

Brown Watson

England.

THE COOPER family lived on a small farm. There were Mr. and Mrs. Cooper, Big Brother Jim, and Little Brother Tommy who was six – and there was Nubbins.

Nubbins was Mr. Cooper's only horse. He worked very hard. He pulled the plough and the hay cart and did all the other jobs that a horse has to do on a farm.

Nubbins was happy. He had lived with the Coopers nearly all his life, and all the Coopers liked him, especially Tommy.

Tommy came to the barn every day after Nubbins' work was finished and always brought him an apple or a lump of sugar. Big Brother Jim gave him fresh water and plenty of oats.

One day a terrible thing happened. As Mr. Cooper and Nubbins were returning from the field for dinner, Brother Jim came running to meet them, shouting, "Oh, Dad, the new tractor is here! Come and see!"

Of course Nubbins had never seen a tractor before. He wondered what it was. When they reached the farm-yard, there it stood – a great,

shiny, red thing with big
wheels at the back and little
wheels in front. And what a
fuss everyone was making
about it! Tommy was climbing
all over it, and Jim was giving
it a drink of water. Why, Jim

was the one who had always brought Nubbins a drink when he came home! Today, no one paid any attention to Nubbins, not even Tommy. Old Nubbins felt hurt and slowly set off towards the barn.

That evening Nubbins heard Mr. Cooper and the tractor returning from the field. Jim and Tommy were with him. Mr. Cooper drove it straight into the barn and stopped next to Nubbins' stall.

"How dreadful!" thought Nubbins, kicking and neighing loudly.

Mr. Cooper and the boys rushed over to calm him. At last, as they were closing the

barn door, he heard Mr. Cooper say, "Jim, I suppose we'll have to sell Old Nubbins. We don't need him now that we have the tractor."

"Oh, Dad," cried Tommy,

"Don't sell Old Nubbins! He's my friend. Give him to me, and he and I will help you with the work. I'm big enough now."

Mr. Cooper smiled down at Tommy's eager face and said,

"Well, son, we'll see."

As the weeks passed, Nubbins became more unhappy. From the pasture he could see Mr. Cooper and the tractor ploughing the fields and cutting the corn. Tommy was his only companion these days.

"Oh, Nubbins," Tommy whispered in his ear, "I wish Dad would give you to me for my very own."

How Nubbins wished it, too!

He did not want to leave the pleasant farm.

One morning in the haymaking season Mr. Cooper came to the barn to get the tractor as usual. But a strange thing happened. The tractor refused to start. Nubbins watched as Jim and Mr. Cooper worked and cranked and fussed. But no matter what they did, it would

not move, it would not roar, it would not even cough.

"Well, this is a fine thing!" exclaimed Mr. Cooper. "Just when I have so much work to do, too! You'll have to call the garage, Jim."

Just then Tommy came running in. "Dad, I think you'll have to use Old Nubbins, won't you?"

"Yes," decided Mr. Cooper. "I think we will, Tommy, and

you'll have to come along and
help in Jim's place while he is
getting the tractor mended."

Nubbins was so happy he
could hardly hold still long

enough for Mr. Cooper to get his harness on him. It was good to be back at work again. He worked hard in the field all day, and so did Tommy.

That evening, on their way

home from the field, Mr. Cooper said, "Tommy, you and Nubbins were a big help to me today. I think I won't sell Old Nubbins after all. He will be your horse from now on, and the two of you can work that field down by the pasture. Would you like that?"

"Oh, thanks, Dad! That's great!" shouted Tommy, patting Nubbins' neck and dancing up and down.

Nubbins had never learned to dance, but he stepped pretty high as he trotted into the barn that night. Now he didn't mind having the red tractor to share his barn, because at last he was Tommy's very own horse and there was plenty of work for them all.